SNOW WHITE

Louis Weber, C.E.O.
Publications International, Ltd.
7373 North Cicero Avenue
Lincolnwood, Illinois 60646

Manufactured in U.S.A.

8 7 6 5 4 3 2 1

ISBN: 0–7853–1032–0

Cover Illustration by Kenny Yamada

Illustrations by Gary Torrisi

Contributing Writer: Dorothea Goldenberg

PUBLICATIONS INTERNATIONAL, LTD.

Once there was a young princess whose skin was so pale and lovely she was called Snow White. Her life would have been wonderful, but her wicked and vain stepmother the queen treated her cruelly.

Every day, the queen would look into her magic mirror and ask who the most beautiful woman in the kingdom was. The mirror always answered, "You may be cruel. You may be mean. But you are also the fairest, my queen."

But one day, when Snow White had grown up, the mirror gave quite a different answer. "You are indeed cruel. You are indeed mean. But Snow White is now the fairest, my queen." The vain queen flew into a terrible, shrieking rage. Because she could not stand to know there was someone in the kingdom more beautiful than she, the queen banished Snow White to the forest.

Alone deep in the woods, Snow White began to cry. She was hungry, tired, frightened, and lost. A friendly blue jay heard her sobs. Looking into her heart, as all birds can do, he saw that she was kind and good, and so he decided to help her. He fluttered softly around her head to get her attention, and then led her to a small cottage tucked into a hillside.

Looking inside, Snow White saw a table set for seven. But everything on the table was very tiny. She was so hungry she did not stop to wonder about the odd table settings. She just helped herself to a little food from each plate.

Going into the next room, Snow White found seven neat little beds all in a row. She was so tired that she stretched out across them and fell asleep.

Soon after, the seven dwarfs who lived in the cottage came home. They had spent the day mining gold and diamonds deep in the mountain. They were amazed to find the princess in their cottage. When they woke Snow White, she told them her sad story.

The dwarfs were touched by the young princess's tale. They decided to help her. The eldest dwarf said, "Stay here with us. We will see that you are safe."

Back at the castle, the queen was still in a rage. Whenever she asked the mirror who was the prettiest, she heard, "You are wicked, you are cruel, and you are a beauty rare. But Snow White, deep in the woods, is easily the most fair."

Furious, the queen decided to kill Snow White. She dressed as a peddler, prepared a poison comb, and hurried off. The queen raged through the forest like a storm, breaking young saplings and stomping over wildflower beds.

She came upon Snow White working in the garden outside the cottage. With a sweet, sly smile the queen offered her the comb. Snow White took the pretty comb and put it in her hair. Instantly, she fell into a deep sleep.

When the dwarfs returned from their day's work, they found Snow White lying in the garden. They feared she was dead.

"The wicked queen must have found her and done this," said the youngest dwarf sadly. He reached down to stroke her hair, and as he did he knocked the comb loose. Snow White awoke at once and thanked him. She broke the poison comb into many small pieces.

When the queen returned home, she excitedly asked the mirror who was fairest in the land. To her great surprise, the mirror said, "Despite your truly evil plan, Snow White is still the fairest in our land." The queen shook with anger.

The queen made a basket of poisonous red apples and returned to the cottage the next day, disguised as a peasant woman. Snow White was again working in the garden, and the jealous queen offered her one of the apples.

"Why thank you," said Snow White. "I am hungry and those apples look delicious."

She raised the apple to her lips and took a small bite. Immediately, she fell to the ground, and the queen hurried away laughing.

Now that she was sure Snow White was dead, the evil queen rushed back to the castle. She hurried up the steps to stand in front of her magic mirror and once again asked, "Mirror Mirror on the wall, now who is fairest of us all?"

The mirror replied, "Gone is the beauty of Snow White, and you are the fairest in my sight." There seemed to be just a hint of sadness in its voice.

The queen didn't notice any change in the mirror's voice. Instead she let out a long, shrill laugh at the success of her plan.

The dwarfs returned home that evening to find Snow White lying on the ground. This time, they could not wake her. With tears in their eyes, they laid her still body on a soft bed of rose petals and moss. Then they sat down to watch over her.

In time, a young prince riding in the forest came upon them. "What a strange sight," he thought.

He stopped his horse and stepped down. Kneeling next to the bed so that he could see her face more clearly, the prince was overwhelmed by Snow White's great beauty and the sweet, kind expression on her face. He fell in love instantly.

"How sad," the prince said softly, "that when I find my true love at last, I cannot marry her."

As the dwarfs looked on, the prince raised Snow White's head, for he longed to be closer to her. As he did so, the piece of apple fell from her mouth and she awoke. Since she had not swallowed the poison, the apple did not kill her.

Snow White looked up at the prince's face and saw that his eyes were filled with love for her. At that moment, she too fell in love. Joyfully, the two smiled at each other.

When the queen asked her mirror who was fairest on that day, the mirror answered, "Oh queen you are a beauty rare, but the bride Snow White will always be more fair."

While the queen raged, the dwarfs celebrated Snow White's awakening. And the very next day, Snow White and the prince were married right there in the dwarfs' garden.